A BIG RED SLED

PEARSON

Glenview, Illinois • Boston, Massachusetts • Chandler, Arizona
Shoreview, Minnesota • Upper Saddle River, New Jersey

2

I go fast on snow.
I go, go, go!

 I zoom from here.
I zoom to the end!

4

I slip from the end!
I drop! Help!

5

I hit the sign.
It can bend.

Look! I am a sled!
I am a big red sled!

8